# TRICK A TRACKER

First published in the United States of America by
Philomel Books, a division of The Putnam Publishing Group,
200 Madison Avenue, New York, N.Y., 10016, 1981.
First published in Great Britain by Victor Gollancz Ltd,
London, 1981. All rights reserved. Except for use in
a review, the reproduction or utilization of this work
in any form is forbidden without the written permission
of the publisher. Printed in Hong Kong.

**Library of Congress Cataloging in Publication Data**

Foreman, Michael, 1938–
   Trick a tracker.

   SUMMARY: In order to foil hunters, the animals
create an ingenious device which disguises their
tracks.
   [1. Animal tracks—Fiction.   2. Skateboarding—
Fiction.   3. Animals—Fiction]   I. Title.
PZ7.F7583TS   1981        [E]        81-293
ISBN 0-399-20820-8                AACR1
ISBN 0-399-61185-1 (lib. bdg.)

# TRICK A TRACKER

## MICHAEL FOREMAN

PHILOMEL BOOKS

New York

Long ago, in the springtime of the world, people
began to be beastly to the other beasts.

They rushed shouting through the world and chased the
animals. When the animals hid, the hunters followed their
tracks to their dens and hideaways.

They thumped their chests and cried,
"We great hunters!"

The hunters got so good at following tracks that
even in their secret places animals were not safe.
But some of the animals were very clever,
and worked out ways to trick the trackers.

But those with short tails had to walk backwards
and didn't notice the traps in their way.

First they made brushes so that they could wipe
out their tracks. These worked well enough for
those animals with long tails.

So the animals decided to give up brushing, which was slow, and invented a fast way of hiding their tracks.

Running shoes were made with strange patterns on the soles.

But the little animals still made little marks, and the
bigger animals made bigger marks and took longer strides.
The trackers were not confused for long.

The animals tried to change this by wearing the same
size shoes, and those with long legs tried to walk
with small steps.

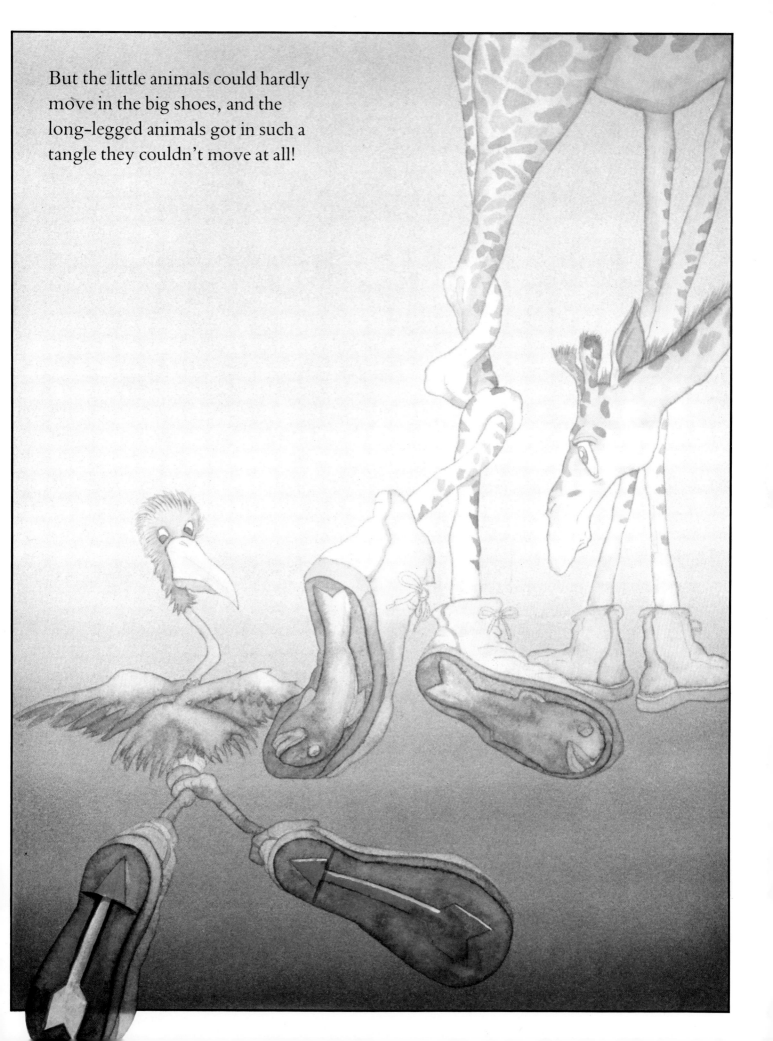

But the little animals could hardly move in the big shoes, and the long-legged animals got in such a tangle they couldn't move at all!

Then the wisest animals made plans which were to change their tracks, change their lives, and even change the world. . . .

The animals stayed up all night sawing and hammering and painting and eating cheese and pickle sandwiches. They sang lots of songs to stay awake, and at dawn their work was complete.

There was great excitement at the trial run.

Now the animals could travel at great speed, and the
trackers could not tell if they were coming or going.

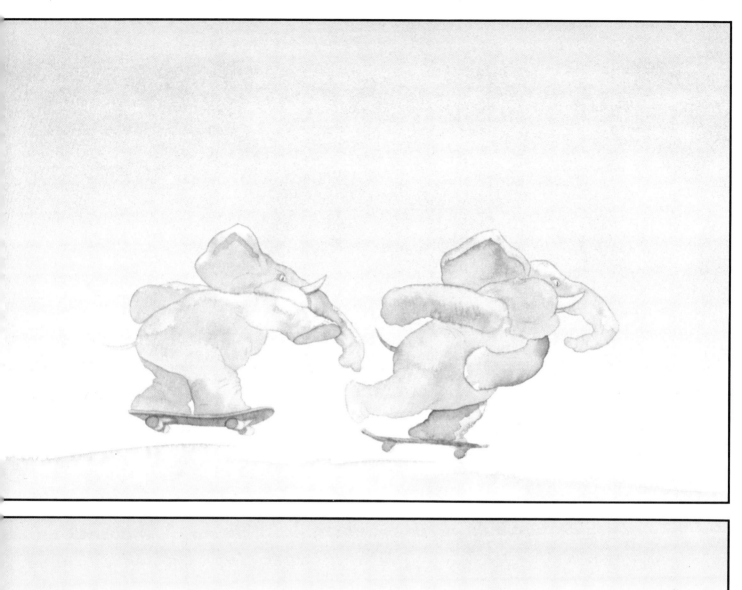

On hard ground the tracks were the same whether
made by the largest elephant or the smallest frog.

On soft ground heavier animals left deeper tracks,
so small animals travelled together to make their
tracks deeper to confuse the trackers.

The animals became so fast and skilful that
they began to frighten the trackers.

With a great whoosh, speeding groups of animals
would suddenly charge, sending the trackers
running in all directions.

News of this great invention spread around the world and
the animals were invited to distant lands to perform.

Everywhere they went, great stadiums were built
so that the crowds could see their heroes race
and do all kinds of tricks.

More and more of the animals wanted to join in,
and even some of the trackers wanted to learn.

Obstacle courses were put up to make it more fun.

Sometimes the obstacles looked like the old trackers,
a joke hugely enjoyed by all the animals.

Later, stadiums were built in far off mountain
places for daring downhill races.

A mouse could show that she was as brave as a lion,
a tortoise as quick as a hare.

But soon the trackers began to be beastly again. They built great trucks so they could all rush shouting through the world once more.

The faster they went, the more they shouted. They built trucks and wagons of every description, each one bigger and faster than the last.

They built roads and great tunnels and bridges so they could go even faster.

They were no longer trackers—they were truck drivers, coach drivers, car drivers, motorcyclists, speed cops, road hogs.

They still rushed shouting through the world, but so fast
that they could look neither to the right nor the left.

They forgot all about the animals.

The animals went back to their old ways in the deep forests
and wild places.

Sometimes, now, they sit with their young ones on sunny hills
and watch the people rushing by.

"Don't worry," the old animals say. "The trackers have tricked
themselves this time. They're too busy chasing each other to
bother chasing us."